BLUMPOE THE GRUMPOE MEETS ARNOLD THE CAT

by Jean Davies Okimoto
Illustrated by Howie Schneider

Little, Brown and Company
Boston Toronto London

For Edie

J.D.O.

Text copyright © 1990 by Jean Davies Okimoto
Illustrations copyright © 1990 by Howie Schneider

First edition

Library of Congress Cataloging-in-Publication Data

Okimoto, Jean Davies.
    Blumpoe the grumpoe meets Arnold the cat / Jean Davies
Okimoto; illustrated by Howie Schneider.
      p. cm.
    Summary: A grumpy old man and a shy young cat form an unlikely friendship at a Minnesota inn which provides its guests with a cat for the night.
  ISBN 0-316-63811-0
  1. Anderson House (Wabasha, Minn.) — Juvenile fiction.
[1. Anderson House (Wabasha, Minn.) — Fiction. 2. Hotels, motels, etc. — Fiction. 3. Cats — Fiction.] I Schneider, Howie, 1930– ill. II. Title.
PZ7.0415Ar   1989
[E] — dc19   88-31436
                                                   CIP
                                                    AC

Joy Street Books are published by Little, Brown and Company (Inc.)

10 9 8 7 6 5 4 3 2 1

WOR

*Published simultaneously in Canada
by Little, Brown & Company (Canada) Limited*

Printed in the United States of America

Horace P. Blumpoe was a grump. Everyone in his neighborhood thought so. They all called him Blumpoe the Grumpoe.

"Wanda Huggins, I'm going to report you!" he growled at the paper girl whenever his newspaper didn't land exactly in the middle of his front porch.

"You dented my can!" he yelled at Norman, the garbage man.

"I expect my mail at three o'clock sharp!" he fussed at Roger, the postman.

Almost everyone knew better than to ring his doorbell on Halloween.

The only things Horace P. Blumpoe wasn't grumpy about were his sister, Edith, whom he visited every year in Saint Cloud, Minnesota, and his dog, Raymond. But Raymond had died at the end of the summer and since then Mr. Blumpoe had gotten crankier than ever.

Edith called and tried to cheer him up. "When you get here, Horace, we can look for another dog for you."

"No dog could measure up, Edith. It's no use. But I am looking forward to seeing you."

As always, Mr. Blumpoe planned to leave for Edith's on November 9. He got up bright and early but when he climbed into the shower, he couldn't get the temperature exactly right. He got so grouchy that he slammed the shower door shut and wrote nasty words on the steam-covered mirror.

Later, while he was making his lunch for the trip, Mr. Blumpoe examined the chunky peanut butter. "Why, there are hardly any chunks!" Even though it would mean a late start, he sat down to write the company a letter of complaint.

On the way to Edith's, Horace's old car began sputtering and steaming. He had gotten only as far as Wabasha when it broke down.

"What do you mean, you can't have it fixed until morning?" he growled at George Potter, the owner of the gas station.

"There's a nice hotel right on Main Street," said George. "It's called the Anderson House."

It began to snow as Horace trudged around the block. By the time he got to the hotel, he was not only very grumpy, he was very cold and very wet.

"My name is Horace P. Blumpoe," he announced to the desk clerk through chattering teeth. "I'm on my way to Saint Cloud and I'm stuck here while my car is being fixed. I will need a room for the night."

"Very good, sir. Room Thirty-three is available. By the way, help yourself to a cookie."

"I'm not hungry," Horace muttered. He hadn't felt like eating much of anything since Raymond died. He didn't even notice the smell of home-baked apple brandy pie coming from the kitchen.

"Well, perhaps you'd like a cat this evening?"

"A what?"

"A cat. Many of our guests miss their pets or aren't able to have pets of their own. They adopt a cat for their stay. We have nineteen cats who live here at Anderson House."

"Of course I don't want a cat! I thought this was a hotel, not a kennel!" Horace grabbed his room key and stomped off.

Meanwhile, the other guests were going into Room 19 to adopt cats for the night. A Scotch Tape salesperson from Saint Paul picked Aloysius. A dentist from Decatur picked Morris, a judge from Green Bay picked Ginger, a bachelor farmer from Lake Wobegon picked Fred, and a furrier from Grosse Point picked Peanuts. A wallpaper hanger from Waukegan picked Debbie, a taxidermist from Kokomo picked Pepper, a saxophonist from Sault Sainte Marie picked Tom-Tom, and some twins from Hibbing picked Tiger.

By six o'clock all the cats had been picked. All except for one — Arnold. Arnold never got picked. Arnold wasn't mean. He didn't bite or scratch or claw, and he used the litter box properly every time. He was a bit on the scrawny side, but that wasn't the reason Arnold never got picked, either. Arnold was shy. Very, very shy.

Gazing out the window at the snowstorm, Arnold thought. "I can't go spending my life in the corner just hoping to get picked. What I need to do," he decided, "is find someone who needs me. Since no one comes to me — I'll have to go to them."

Arnold jumped down and set off for the lobby. "Be brave," he told himself, as he tiptoed down the long hall. He scooted into the lobby and hid. His heart was pounding.

Arnold watched the guests going into the dining room. None of them looked as if they needed him. Then he noticed a man who was by himself. "That's got to be the one," thought Arnold. He trotted behind Mr. Blumpoe and followed him into the dining room.

Horace P. Blumpoe ordered chicken noodle soup and sighed. Whenever he ate chicken noodle soup at home he used to leave a few noodles for Raymond. Now there was no one to leave a noodle for.

When he was finished, Mr. Blumpoe put his spoon down, and headed upstairs. On the way he couldn't help noticing the other guests playing with their cats. "Silly people — ridiculous!" he muttered.

Arnold trotted along behind, peeking into all the rooms as he went. "How wonderful it must be," he thought, as he saw Princess with the electrician from Evanston, and Hainey with the dermatologist from Oshkosh. He'd heard stories of how guests saved their cats little pieces of lobster, chicken, trout, or ham pot pie from the dinner table.

"Soon I will have a guest, too," Arnold thought happily.

But by the time he got to the end of the hall, Mr. Blumpoe had gone into his room and closed the door.

Arnold could hear the girls in Room 32 giggling as they dressed Tiger in their doll clothes. Horace P. Blumpoe could hear them too.

"Pipe down!" he barked, opening the door to his room.

"This is my chance!" thought Arnold. He scooted into the room and hid under the bed.

Horace P. Blumpoe turned out the light and pulled the covers tight around him, but his feet were freezing. After a moment he got up to put on his socks.

Mr. Blumpoe tossed and turned. He hated strange beds. He tried sleeping on his back. He tried sleeping on his stomach. He tried sleeping on his side curled up like a ball. He wiggled his toes, but they felt like ice. He plumped up his pillow. He pulled the quilt over his ears. Finally, he found a nice little spot in the middle of the mattress and began to doze off.

Arnold peered out from under the bed. He practiced some friendly faces and then slowly crept out. He inched his way up onto the bed, tiptoed across the quilt, and settled down.

"Hmmmmm," Blumpoe sighed as his feet began to warm up. He yawned, stretched his legs, and turned over on his side.

He opened one eye.
Then he opened the other eye.
Then he sat straight up in bed.
"WHAT ARE YOU DOING HERE?"

Arnold looked at Mr. Blumpoe. He tried to smile his best welcoming smile.

"Scat! Out with you!" Mr. Blumpoe waved his arms.

"Oh, bosh," Blumpoe grumbled as he struggled out of bed. He stomped to the door, opened it, and pointed firmly toward the hall. "Scat, cat!"

Arnold walked to the head of the bed and sat on the pillow. "What is this nice man trying to say to me?" he wondered.

Blumpoe grabbed his slipper and slashed the air. "Out! Out!"
Arnold lay down and looked happily at his new companion.

Mr. Blumpoe waved the slipper at Arnold. "OUT, OUT, DARNED CAT!"
he shrieked.

Arnold leaped on top of the dresser. Blumpoe swung at him again. "Oh, dear," thought Arnold. "I don't think he likes me."

He fled to the bathroom and hid behind the tub. Blumpoe charged after him, but Arnold jumped over him and . . .

darted up the drapes.

Arnold fled to safety.

Finally, Horace P. Blumpoe limped off to bed. He lay there with his freezing feet, too tired to move.

Underneath the bed, Arnold imagined all his friends with their guests, all cuddled up, cozy and nice. He took a deep breath. Very lightly and very carefully he jumped on the bed.

Horace P. Blumpoe opened one eye. "Scat, cat," he mumbled.
    Arnold sat on his feet.

Mr. Blumpoe didn't move.
So Arnold lay down.

Mr. Blumpoe opened one eye.
He looked at Arnold.
    Arnold curled around his feet.

Blumpoe closed his eye.
Arnold began to purr.

Blumpoe began to snore.

Snore and purr. Snore and purr.

Arnold crept up the bed and snuggled in the crook of Blumpoe's arm. Blumpoe dreamed of homemade chicken noodle soup.

In the morning, Blumpoe sat up in bed and stretched while Arnold quietly crawled onto his lap. Sleepily, Mr. Blumpoe stroked Arnold's fur. He could smell Dutch cinnamon rolls baking in the kitchen and his mouth began to water.

"Let's see what kind of day it is, cat," he said and carried Arnold to the window. They looked out at the sun sparkling on the snow on the banks of the Mississippi River.

Arnold sat and watched Mr. Blumpoe get dressed. He especially liked seeing the shaving cream on Mr. Blumpoe's face. Next, Arnold watched Mr. Blumpoe pack.

"If you fold your clothes right, cat, they won't be so wrinkled when you get where you're going."

When Mr. Blumpoe left his room, Arnold was one step behind him. "What is the name of this cat?" Mr. Blumpoe asked the maid, who told him.

At breakfast, Arnold sat under Mr. Blumpoe's chair. Mr. Blumpoe saved him a piece of cinnamon roll.

When they'd finished, it was time for Mr. Blumpoe to check out. "I would like to reserve a room for the nineteenth of November on my way back from Saint Cloud," he said, helping himself to a cookie at the front desk. "And, I uh — I would also like to reserve a cat."

"Any particular cat, sir?"

"I would like Arnold."